GAL 4/16

2 3 AUG 2018

1 2 OCT 2019
1 3 MAR 2019

Re   lly

Please return this book on or before the date shown above. To
renew go to www.essex.gov.uk/libraries, ring 0345 603 7628 or
go to any Essex library.

Essex County Council

To my really really brave friend Paul d'Auria – K.G.
For Jon – N.S.

DAISY: REALLY, REALLY
A RED FOX BOOK 978 1 782 95646 4
First published in Great Britain by The Bodley Head, an imprint of Random House Children's Publishers UK
A Penguin Random House Company

The Bodley Head edition published 2002
Red Fox edition published 2003
This edition published 2016

13 5 7 9 10 8 6 4 2

Penguin Random House is committed to a sustainable future for our business, our readers and our planet.
This book is made from Forest Stewardship Council® certified paper.

FSC
www.fsc.org

MIX
Paper from
responsible sources
FSC® C018179

Red Fox Books are published by Random House Children's Publishers UK,
61–63 Uxbridge Road, London W5 5SA

www.randomhousechildrens.co.uk www.randomhouse.co.uk

Addresses for companies within The Random House Group Limited can be found at: www.randomhouse.co.uk/offices.htm

THE RANDOM HOUSE GROUP Limited Reg. No. 954009

A CIP catalogue record for this book is available from the British Library.

Printed in China

DAISY
Really, Really

Kes Gray & Nick Sharratt

RED FOX

Daisy was very excited.
She'd never had a babysitter before.

Daisy's *mum* was very late.
"Daisy meet Angela, Angela meet Daisy!" said Daisy's *mum*,
kissing Daisy on the forehead and then running down
the path to the taxi waiting outside.

Angela the babysitter closed the front door and smiled at Daisy. "Why are you eating paper?" she asked.

"I'm not eating paper," said Daisy.
"Really?" said Angela.
"Really, really," fibbed Daisy.

"You must be hungry," said Angela.
"What do you usually have
for tea?"
"Ice-cream and chips," said Daisy.
"Really?" said Angela.
"Really, really," fibbed Daisy.

"Have you ever had a babysitter before?" asked Angela.

"Hundreds!" said Daisy.

"Really?" said Angela.

"Really, really," fibbed Daisy.

"Would you like a glass of milk?" asked Angela.

"I'm only allowed lemonade," said Daisy.

"Really?" said Angela.

"Really, really," fibbed Daisy.

"What time do you usually
go to bed?" asked Angela.
"Midnight at the earliest,"
said Daisy.
"Really?" said Angela.
"Really, really," fibbed Daisy.

"Do you need to have a bath?" asked Angela.

"I don't get dirty," said Daisy.

"Really?" said Angela.

"Really, really," fibbed Daisy.

"What time do you put your pyjamas on?" asked Angela.
"I always sleep in my clothes," said Daisy.
"Really?" said Angela.
"Really, really," fibbed Daisy.

"Shall we sit down and do some reading?" asked Angela.

"My *mum* prefers it if I play games," said Daisy.

"What sort of games?" asked Angela.

"Bouncing on the settee and sliding on the table," said Daisy, "until ten o'clock."

"Really?" said Angela.

"Really, really," fibbed Daisy.

"Then we watch videos till midnight," said Daisy.

"Really?" said Angela.

"Really, really," fibbed Daisy.

At midnight Daisy heard a taxi pull up outside her house.
"I'm feeling very sleepy all of a sudden," said Daisy,
jumping off the sofa and scooting upstairs to bed.

Angela opened the front door and
Daisy's *mum* tiptoed in.
"Hello Angela," whispered Daisy's *mum*.
"Has Daisy been a good girl?
She did give *you* my note didn't she?
She did have a proper tea
didn't she? She did have a
bath and wash her hair?
She did put clean pyjamas
on didn't she? She was in
bed by eight wasn't she?
And she didn't charge
around the house like
a mad thing did she?"

Angela put her hands behind her back and crossed her fingers.

"She's been as good as gold," said Angela. "She's been a little angel."

"Really?" asked Daisy's mum.

"Really, really," fibbed Angela.

DAISY

LITTLE TROUBLE

There are many more
Daisy picture books to discover:

- Daisy: 006 and a Bit
- Daisy: Eat Your Peas
- Daisy: Tiger Ways
- Daisy: You Do!
- Daisy: Yuk!
- Super Daisy

BIG TROUBLE

Join Daisy on these
adventures for older readers:

- Daisy and the Trouble with Giants
- Daisy and the Trouble with Kittens
- Daisy and the Trouble with Life
- Daisy and the Trouble with Zoos

. . . AND MANY MORE!